Dear Parents and Educators,

Welcome to Penguin Young Readers! As parents and educators, you know that each child develops at his or her own pace—in terms of speech, critical thinking, and, of course, reading. Penguin Young Readers recognizes this fact. As a result, each Penguin Young Readers book is assigned a traditional easy-to-read level (1–4) as well as a Guided Reading Level (A–P). Both of these systems will help you choose the right book for your child. Please refer to the back of each book for specific leveling information. Penguin Young Readers features esteemed authors and illustrators, stories about favorite characters, fascinating nonfiction, and more!

Pearl and Wagner: Two Good Friends

LEVEL 3

GUIDED READING LEVEL **K**

This book is perfect for a **Transitional Reader** who:
• can read multisyllable and compound words;
• can read words with prefixes and suffixes;
• is able to identify story elements (beginning, middle, end, plot, setting, characters, problem, solution); and
• can understand different points of view.

Here are some **activities** you can do during and after reading this book:
• Identify the problem(s) and solution(s) in the story.
• Make Predictions: What will the characters do next?
• Discuss the different settings in the story.
• List all of the words in the story that have an -ed ending. Write the root word next to each word with an -ed ending.

word with an -ed ending	root word
taped	tape
looked	look
slipped	slip

Remember, sharing the love of reading with a child is the best gift you can give!

—Bonnie Bader, EdM, and Katie Carella, EdM
   Penguin Young Readers program

*Penguin Young Readers are leveled by independent reviewers applying the standards developed by Irene Fountas and Gay Su Pinnell in *Matching Books to Readers: Using Leveled Books in Guided Reading*, Heinemann, 1999.

For Bud Wilson, my favorite ham, and for
Henry Shaw, who is toadally cool—KM

To the electrical scientists of Hampden
Meadows School—RWA

Penguin Young Readers
Published by the Penguin Group
Penguin Group (USA) Inc., 375 Hudson Street, New York, New York 10014, USA
Penguin Group (Canada), 90 Eglinton Avenue East, Suite 700,
Toronto, Ontario M4P 2Y3, Canada (a division of Pearson Penguin Canada Inc.)
Penguin Books Ltd., 80 Strand, London WC2R 0RL, England
Penguin Group Ireland, 25 St. Stephen's Green, Dublin 2, Ireland (a division of Penguin Books Ltd.)
Penguin Group (Australia), 250 Camberwell Road, Camberwell, Victoria 3124,
Australia (a division of Pearson Australia Group Pty. Ltd.)
Penguin Books India Pvt. Ltd., 11 Community Centre, Panchsheel Park, New Delhi—110 017, India
Penguin Group (NZ), 67 Apollo Drive, Rosedale, North Shore 0632, New Zealand
(a division of Pearson New Zealand Ltd.)
Penguin Books (South Africa) (Pty.) Ltd., 24 Sturdee Avenue, Rosebank,
Johannesburg 2196, South Africa

Penguin Books Ltd., Registered Offices: 80 Strand, London WC2R 0RL, England

The Library of Congress has cataloged the Dial edition under the following Control Number: 2002000339

ISBN 978-0-448-45690-4   10 9 8 7 6 5 4 3 2 1

Pearl and Wagner
Two Good Friends

by Kate McMullan
pictures by R. W. Alley

Penguin Young Readers
An Imprint of Penguin Group (USA) Inc.

Contents

Ms. Star's Class · Rm 6

Chapter 1
The Robot

Everyone in Ms. Star's class
was talking about the Science Fair.
"I am going to make a robot,"
said Pearl.
"I am going to win a prize,"
said Wagner.

Pearl got to work.

She taped up the flaps
of a great big box.

She cut a hole in the top.

Then she cut a hole in the lid
of a shoe box.

She glued the shoe box lid
to the top of the great big box.

Wagner held the boxes together
while the glue dried.
"Maybe I will make
a walkie-talkie," he said.

Pearl punched a hole
in one end of the shoe box.
She stuck string through the hole.
She tied the string in a knot.
"Maybe I will make a brain
out of clay," said Wagner.
"Cool," said Pearl.
She drew eyes and a nose
on the shoe box.

Wagner looked at the shoe box.

"The eyes are too small," he said.

Pearl made the eyes bigger.

"Maybe I will make a rocket,"

said Wagner. "*Vrooom!* Blast off!"

Pearl put the shoe box onto the lid.

"There!" she said. "Finished!"

Pearl pulled the string.

The robot's mouth opened.

She threw in a wad of paper.

Then she let go of the string.

The robot's mouth shut.

"Wow!" said Wagner.

"A trash-eating robot!"

"Let's see what everyone has made,"
said Ms. Star.

"Uh-oh," said Wagner.

He had not made anything yet.

Lulu raised her hand.

"I made a walkie-talkie," she said.

"I was going to do that!" said Wagner.

"I made paper airplanes," said Bud.

"This chart shows how far they flew."

Wagner slapped his head.

"Why didn't *I* think of that?"

Henry showed how to get
electricity from a potato.
"Henry is a brain," said Pearl.

"Pearl?" Wagner said.
"Remember how I held the boxes
together while the glue dried?"
"I remember," said Pearl.
"Remember how I told you
to give the robot bigger eyes?"
asked Wagner.
Pearl nodded. "I remember."

"Your turn, Pearl," said Ms. Star.

"I made a trash-eating robot,"
said Pearl.

She looked at Wagner.

He was slumped down in his seat.

"Wagner and I made it together,"
said Pearl.

Wagner sat right up again.

Pearl pulled the robot's string.

She pulled too hard.

The robot's head fell off.

"Uh-oh," said Wagner.

"I guess you two friends have
more work to do," said Ms. Star.
"I guess so," said Pearl.
"But I don't mind,
because Wagner and I
will do all of the work together."
"Uh-oh," said Wagner.

Chapter 2
The Science Fair

On Science Fair Day

Pearl and Wagner were still working

on their robot.

Pearl stretched rubber bands.

She held them tight.

Wagner stapled them

onto the shoe box and the lid.

"That should do it," he said.

Look at
the ANTS
The ants dig and
dig and dig to
make tunnels. It's
a good life

Plants love music
See the effect of
Music on planted in
the pot marigolds.

Pearl and Wagner hurried
to the gym with their robot.
They passed a boy with an ant village.
They passed a girl playing music
for plants.

They passed Henry.

He had his electric potato

hooked up to a tiny Ferris wheel.

Pearl and Wagner set up their robot.

A judge came over.

"Watch this," said Pearl.

Pearl pulled the robot's string.

Nothing happened.

She pulled harder.

The robot's mouth popped open.

The rubber bands flew everywhere.

"Yikes!" said the judge.

"Oh, no!" said Wagner.

"There goes our prize!"

"We are not quite ready,"

Pearl told the judge.

"I will come back in five minutes,"

said the judge.

"I have more rubber bands
in my desk," said Pearl.
She raced off to get them.
Wagner tapped his foot.
He bit his nails.
Pearl was taking forever!
The judge would be back any second.
He had to *do* something.

Wagner looked around.

No one was watching him.

He pulled the tape off the big box.

He opened the back of the robot

and slipped inside.

The judge came back.

She did not see Pearl and Wagner.

She started to leave.

"WAIT!" said the robot.

"Oh, my stars!" said the judge.

"A talking robot!"

Just then Pearl came back.

"YOU HAVE A NICE SMILE,"
the robot was telling the judge.

"AND SUCH PRETTY EYES."

"Do you think so?" said the judge.

Pearl could not believe her ears.

"Your robot is so smart!"
said the judge.
"How does it work?"
"Uh . . ." said Pearl.
"It is hard to explain."

The judge opened the robot's mouth.

She looked inside.

"Hi there!" said Wagner.

"Uh-oh," said Pearl.

The judge gave out the prizes.

The girl who played music for plants
won first prize.

Henry and his electric potato
won second prize.

The trash-eating robot
did not win any prize at all.

"I was only trying to help,"
Wagner told Pearl.

"I know," said Pearl.

"You are a good friend, Wagner.
And you were a
pretty good robot, too."

Chapter 3
The New Boots

Wagner was waiting
to walk to school with Pearl.
Pearl came running toward him.
CLOMP! CLOMP! CLOMP!
"Wagner!" she called.
"Look at my new green boots!"

Wagner looked.

He thought the boots were *awful*.

"Do you like them?" asked Pearl.

"Well . . ." said Wagner.

"Well, what?" said Pearl.

"Do you like my new boots?

Or don't you?"

"I don't, Pearl," said Wagner.

"Your new boots are too green.

They look like big fat pickles.

And they make way too much noise."

Pearl gasped.

Then she ran to school by herself.

CLOMP! CLOMP! CLOMP!

Wagner walked to school alone.

That day Pearl worked on spelling
with Bud.

Wagner studied his words by himself.

At math time

Pearl and Henry did flash cards.

They laughed like crazy.

Wagner walked by them.

"I never knew flash cards
were so funny," he said.

Pearl pretended not to hear him.

At recess Pearl let Lulu
try on her left new boot.
"It is dreamy!" said Lulu.
"I know it," said Pearl.
"Even if a certain somebody
does not think so."

Wagner wanted to make up
with Pearl.
But he did not know how.
He hung by his knees
on the jungle gym.
At last he thought of a way.

Wagner hurried over to Henry.

"I need some help," Wagner told him.

"I'm your man," said Henry.

They ran back into school.

A few minutes later Lulu looked up.

"Hey, Pearl," she said.

"Here comes your robot."

"Oh, that Wagner!" said Pearl.

"He makes me so mad!"

The robot walked up to Pearl.

"WAGNER WANTS ME TO TELL YOU HE IS SORRY," it said.

"Scram, Wagner," said Pearl.

Wagner came up behind Pearl.

He tapped her on the shoulder.

"Yikes!" cried Pearl.

Pearl opened the robot's mouth.

"Hi there!" said Henry.

Henry walked away.

"Pearl?" said Wagner.

"I am sorry I hurt your feelings."

"Have you changed your mind
about my new boots?" asked Pearl.

"No," said Wagner.

"I still do not like your boots.
But *you* like them.
And that is all that matters."

Pearl looked down
at her new green boots.
"I don't like them," she said.
"I *love* them!"

The bell rang.

Recess was over.

Pearl grabbed Wagner's arm.

They ran back into school together.

CLOMP! CLOMP! CLOMP!

Wagner wondered why he had ever
thought that Pearl's new boots
made too much noise.

After recess
Ms. Star's class had art.
Wagner painted a picture
of two good friends together.
"Now *that* should win a prize,"
said Pearl.